The Coveted Beta

Coveted Prey
Book 20

L.V. Lane

Cover design by Three Spires Creative
Cover character art by @NguyenKamZ
Editing by Steph Tashkoff

Contents

Chapter One

Frederick

It has been a year or more since I last saw Alex. We were once very close, first as children and later during our time in the high king's court. More recently, life and circumstances have caused our paths to part.

He's married now, and he and his wife live on a small estate nestled deep within the protection of his brother's kingdom. Their modest home has a cozy charm to it. Ivy creeps over the cream stone walls of the two-story dwelling set against the backdrop of a small wood. There is a small holding to go with it, with arable land, an orchard, grazing for sheep, and a village close by from which he can hire workers for his land. A small formal garden and an orchard, stable blocks, and numerous barns complete the main building complex.

A stablehand is swift to collect my horse, and I'm greeted by Alex and his wife, Clara, on the steps of their home.

I try not to breathe as Clara breaks all decorum and

throws her arms around my neck. "It's so good to see you, Frederick!"

Alex only chuckles and shakes my hand when his wife, now blushing, relinquishes her hold.

"Do you have the letters?" Clara asks, not even pretending she is excited to see me anymore as she searches my riding coat with her eyes, like her sisters' correspondence might appear through her will alone.

I pat myself down, frowning. "Oh dear."

"What? Where are they?"

"Clara!" Alex all but groans. "At least let the man get over the threshold before you accost him for news."

"He promised to bring the letters." She pouts prettily.

"I fear I might have left them back at my residence in the capital," I muse, fighting down laughter at the sudden mutinous set to Clara's jaw.

"No." She shakes her head. "I am not falling for that. Hand over the letters, scoundrel, or you shall be sleeping in the stable without supper."

I like the way she calls me *scoundrel* a little more than I ought.

Alex laughs. "I would come to your defense, but my wife is not known for her leniency where news from her sisters is concerned."

My smirk blooms and I join him in laughter as I take the two letters from my inside pocket with a flourish.

She snatches them from my hand, leans up on her tiptoes to kiss my cheek, and then turns about to disappear back into the house, calling over her shoulder, "He may enter."

My cheek still tingles where her soft lips pressed. "Your sweet wife is magnanimous," I say dryly, dragging my eyes from her ass—I'm confident there is no padding needed in her silk gown.

Alex claps me on the shoulder. "Good to see you, Frederick. Come in and be welcome. I'm sure as soon as Clara has read the letters two or three times, she will remember we have a guest."

Their house is as charming on the inside as it is on the out. Large enough to be comfortable and small enough to be intimate. Clara is beaming after reading the letters—one from each of her sisters, Rebecca and Rosalind. I know how she cherishes news from them, genuine news, for one cannot trust the messengers since her oldest sister came to power and set in motion events that changed all our lives.

I push aside the dark anger I still feel even after the passage of several years.

Not that I still covet the mate I might have had when Rebecca was snatched away, but more that I hate the injustice and damage it did to the rest of their family. Rebecca is happy now, and that comforts me.

But as we enjoy a fine evening meal in their beautiful dining room with the elegant rosewood table and chairs and the crystal candelabra that bespeaks their modest wealth, it is not the omega I almost claimed who captivates me, but her beta sister... Her happily married beta sister, who happens to be my best friend's wife.

Chapter Two

Alex

After the fallout from what happened to Clara's family and the rise of her bitchy older sister Elisa, I knew I had to extract my wife from the insidious elements within her family and society in general. Given how trusting she is by nature, it is my duty as her husband to protect her. Elisa, now a queen, has torn the family apart and set in motion events that led to her father's death and her mother's abdication—her two sisters, who revealed as omegas, suffered terribly at her hands.

Clara is like a precious flower that withers under stress yet blooms under the influence of care and love. What happened to her omega sisters, whom she loves well, has taken a heavy toll. Our modest home and small estate are away from the capital and those terrible events—a place where she can be herself and be cherished.

But it's also good to catch up with an old friend. It reminds us of who we are, the enduring relationships, and what is important.

Smiling, I watch my wife as she dances with Frederick. The alpha towers over her, making my beta wife look almost doll-like in his arms. Dinner is over, and lamps have been lit with the turn toward evening. There is no music playing. My sweet wife expressed the desire for dancing, and Frederick insisted that he would partner her despite the lack of accompaniment. Now, they twirl around the drawing room to some imaginary song as I relax on the couch with my brandy and watch.

She giggles as he spins her around before bringing their dance to a stop. She lays her hand against her heaving breasts.

Gods, I love my wife. How I feel blessed to have been gifted such a sweet angel who does not know a bit of artifice and believes only the best of everyone. What her sister did, the ugliness that surrounded her, broke me on many levels, but most profoundly because it left scars on Clara's gentle soul.

She turns to me, her smile brightening on finding me watching. I am worldly enough to know how things work. I'm a beta; Frederick is an alpha: wealthy, handsome, and civilized enough to make him desirable on every front. I've seen married women make fools of themselves over him, whether their husbands were there or not. Perhaps I ought to feel more threatened by him, yet I am not. There has never been a moment where I could ever doubt Clara's love. It shines in her face and is reflected in her ways every day.

"I think I need a drink after all that dancing," Clara says.

"Let me get you something." I rise, taking her hand to guide her over to a couch. She's pink-cheeked and adorable, her long blonde hair shining in the lamplight and her blue eyes bright.

I wink at Frederick. "You have put a blush on my wife's cheeks."

"Your wife is blessed to be both pretty and fun."

Her blush deepens under his praise. She sips the wine I fetch for her, and we fall into easy conversation, which skirts around Elisa and her rise in the high king's court. Frederick has recently returned from travels. A cousin to the high king, he holds power and influence and knows all matters of importance.

I'm pleased to say that none of his status has destroyed his good nature. He's a man who has demonstrated his integrity many times and in many ways.

"Another brandy?" I ask.

He nods, taking a seat beside my wife.

"Has no woman caught your eye, then, Frederick? Your poor mother must be pining for her first grandchild to spoil," Clara asks, looking up at him.

He huffs out a breath, smirking, as he shakes his head and takes a deep drink of the brandy I pass him. "My mother is not so old and can assuredly wait."

I take the seat opposite, from where I watch them chat amiably about all sorts of gossip from the capital. I am quiet, content to sink into my own thoughts, although these begin to drift in a dangerous direction as I take in the way they look beside each other: how much larger he is compared to her, and how they strike the notes of extremes of masculine and feminine.

I feel lucky that I found her first, for he would have wasted no time claiming her—even though she is a beta.

There might be some who would feel jealous of another man so close to his wife, but that is not the emotion that stirs within me tonight. What I feel is more... curiosity. Before I can curb my thoughts, I have ventured into imagining her underneath him, spread open, her gorgeous body on display. I imagine his heated gaze as he sees what lies beneath her gown for, while my wife is sweet, the Goddess has blessed her with a body made for sin.

"I think I'll call it a night," Clara says, rousing me from the spiral of my fantasy. "I need to write to Rosalind and Rebecca. Also, without me here, you can catch up on everything Frederick won't tell me—I'm sure *someone* has caught his eye..."

Frederick chuckles as she rises to set her empty glass upon the sideboard.

We both rise with her. Frederick performs a gallant bow and kisses the back of her hand. She giggles before offering me a much more intimate and lingering kiss on my cheek.

My dear wife is a little tipsy, it would seem.

"I'll be along shortly."

"Take your time," she says. "You do not see each other often these days. Enjoy yourselves. Talk."

She leaves the room, but her soft scent lingers. When I turn, I find Frederick's eyes on her ass as she sashays out.

A sharp jolt of lust catches me by surprise as the door clicks softly shut.

"You're one lucky bastard," Frederick says, turning back to me, his smile rueful.

"Trust me, I know."

We return to our seats and discuss events as he updates me on Elisa's scheming.

"There are rumors the high king is bedding Elisa behind her alpha's back. Meanwhile, her alpha has gotten a servant with child. Their marriage is all but a sham. Now, they are two dark blights seeking to bring down everything and everyone in their sphere of influence. You did the right thing taking Clara away from her sister," Frederick says with heat. "I've never felt violence toward a woman, but I could happily strangle that bitch."

His words don't even shock me. He is an alpha, after all. Although he presents a refined facade, there is no mistaking what lies beneath it.

Chapter Three

Clara

I am supposed to be replying to my sisters' letters, but the truth is that I find myself distracted. The letters sit before me on my dressing table. I have already read them several times, but even their happy news and talk of growing children and more babies on the way does not hold my attention the way it usually would.

The reason I left the drawing room was not to write letters nor to rest in our bedroom and be soothed by the elegant cream and forest green tones, which I love so much. I took myself away because I needed to; before I did something foolish that I would later regret. Because there is something different about Frederick tonight. Something... unguarded about him. I am sure that the terrible events that have enshrouded my entire family have undoubtedly changed him as much as they've affected me. He should have married my sister, Rebecca, and would have done so but for Elisa's schemes. Frederick searched for a year only to find Rebecca living as a servant among the fallen centaurs.

He offered her his protection and marriage even though she carried a centaur's child; despite knowing it would be loveless when a centaur had already claimed her heart.

She is happy, now, living with the centaur of her dreams, far from here and my oldest sister's cruel ways. If Frederick feels any bitterness toward the events that cost him an omega mate, none of it shows, save I know he shares my husband's hatred for Elisa.

I have always held Frederick in high regard, placing him on a pedestal, never really acknowledging him as a man and alpha. While he searched for Rebecca, I held onto the fantasy that he might find her and return with her as his mate.

Only it didn't work out, and now my younger sister is mated and pregnant with her second babe, while Frederick is very much alone.

From the day he returned to the capital without a mate, I have hoped for him to find his special one—I wish for him to find the happiness he deserves. But I discovered tonight that another part of me has become intrigued in him for totally selfish reasons.

Tonight, I saw a darker version of him, something that had escaped my notice before, something that is just underneath the surface. It should frighten me. And yet, it had a very different effect. As I sit at my dresser, pondering this, I ask myself when this strange feeling started. I can pinpoint the exact moment. We were dancing. And I glanced across at Alex to find him staring at us, his eyes darkening with unmistakable lust.

That heated look ignited a flame inside of me. It made me aware of things I had not been aware of before. Tonight, Frederick was not merely a friend of my husband's, nor the man who might have gone on to mate my sister, but a handsome alpha, powerful and influential, with a sinful sense of humor and a devastating smile.

Women become scandalous in their pursuit of Frederick, whether they are married or not. I won't be such a woman. I love my husband and have no desire to feel another man's hands upon me.

Yet I am sure I would not be having these thoughts on my own. This is all Alex's fault. The way he looked at us together—like he was enjoying it. I try telling myself I misinterpreted the look.

But what else could have made him look at us that way?

Maybe Alex is attracted to Frederick?

No, he wasn't looking at his friend, per se. He was looking at his friend with me.

The second glass of wine was a mistake. I'm hot and flushed. My dress felt uncomfortable across my breasts when I fled under the pretense of letter-writing when it was really to give me time to regain composure.

Frederick is staying for several days. So I must find a way to hide this strange awakening inside me. I've heard of this before: how alphas can impact women, whether an omega or a beta.

None ever influenced me before, and I don't want it now.

I wish I could wipe it away, yet the strange undercurrent of lust has me in a stranglehold as I remove my gown and brush out my hair. Afterward, I stand naked before the mirror. I know Alex loves my body, the flair of my hips, my ample ass, my generous breasts. He loves my hair, too, and often tells me I am beautiful and desirable.

He tells me he loves my ways.

But a tiny part of me remains in reserve, not willing to totally trust what he says, when I have long lived in the shadow of my sisters. Rebecca and Rosalind always had a spark of adventure and flair. As for Elisa, although she is an embittered and cruel woman, no one could dispute her fire. Then there is my other sister, Violet, a purposeful woman driven by intellect and curiosity.

I am nothing like them—any of them—and, more, I take the greatest satisfaction in being Alex's wife. I long to be a mother, but that has not happened yet. By nature, I'm submissive and find great happiness in pleasing people. There was a time when pleasing Elisa gave me joy. Even when she began her cruelty, I continued to be kind to her hoping that my kindness might have some improving effect and counter her growing bitterness when she didn't get with child.

Nothing I did would ever help Elisa. It was a relief when Alex announced we would be leaving the high king's court and taking residence in the country. Our estate was a wedding gift to us from his brother: he downplayed the extent of his generosity by telling us it had been sitting unoccupied for several years.

I have fallen in love with it and the quietness here and my husband all over again. I have found that he is worthy of my loving attention, whereas Elisa is not. With him, I feel nurtured and seen.

I feel loved.

Buoyed by these warm feelings, I move over to my wardrobe to choose something different to wear to bed. Pushing aside one nightgown and then another, my fingers linger on one of the more decadent ones Alex bought for me from a distant empire. It is sheer with bows along the front that cinch the material underneath my breasts.

Yes, this perfectly fits my mood.

I slip it on. It falls to my feet, yet I might as well be

naked. I stand closer to the mirror, tracing my fingers over the areolas of my nipples, visible through the material, and I shiver as the faint touch causes them to tighten.

My cheeks are a little flushed, and my eyes are bright. I've had a little too much to drink, perhaps. But I also believe it's the influence of alpha scent after Frederick held me close.

I was foolish dancing with him, even though it started so innocently—right up until that look in my husband's eyes.

As I slip into the bed, I don't even pretend to sleep. I toy absently with my nipples, brushing my fingertips back and forth over the material, enjoying the bloom of arousal as heat and dampness gather between my thighs. They are talking very late, but I already know what I shall do the moment Alex enters the room.

I'm hoping my husband is congenial to the ardor that clamors in my mind.

Chapter Four

Alex

I expect Clara to be asleep, but my wife lies in bed, awake, waiting for me, with a book lying open across her chest.

She sits up in a sudden rush, and the book drops to the floor with a thud. She doesn't even spare it a glance as she throws back the bedclothes to get down from our bed. "I thought you would never stop talking!"

My heart rate elevates as I see what she wears. My wife has the most scandalous collection of undergarments and nightgowns, the purchase of which I have fully endorsed—if not facilitated myself, for some are wisps of fabric that I have brought her from my travels. The material of this one is so sheer I can see the berry red of her nipples.

Nipping on her lower lip, she steps right up to me and sinks to her knees. Her small hands are on my belt buckle, already tugging impatiently.

A hiss escapes my lips. Clara is not usually this bold. Her chest is heaving as she tugs my pants down and liberates my cock, which is roused to instant hardness by her enthusiasm.

She licks her lips and pauses, my cock mere inches from her mouth, her chest heaving. "Goddess, I'm so sorry. I don't know..." She turns away, a deep blush on her cheeks, although she does not release my cock. "I don't know what came over me, I'm..."

I cup her cheek and slide my fingers into her long hair that tumbles in waves of blonde beauty down her shoulders and back. Gently, I turn her to face me.

"My love, there is not a part of me that does not belong to you. You never need to apologize for this. Ever." My lips tug up. "I believe you can tell I'm enthusiastic about whatever you have in mind."

She nibbles on her lower lip and then, without further hesitation, leans up to swallow the head of my cock.

I huff out a breath and stare up at the ceiling, steeling myself for the impact of her sweet suckling against my flesh. "Gods, Clara. That feels so fucking good."

She hums around my cock. I do not often use coarse language in her presence, but her actions weave a spell upon me. Pretty cheeks hollowed, she takes me down her throat, gagging a little, then shuffling closer on her knees to seek more.

My fingers tighten in her hair. I try to be gentle; I really do. "Angels weep, this feels like heaven. That's my precious wife. Go a little deeper if you can. I know you want to. I'm going to spoil your pussy just as soon as you're done. Would you like that? Would you like me to kiss you there?"

Her answer is to suck deeper, working her hand along my length, lapping, licking, and swirling her tongue around the head until I'm a man hanging on the edge. My balls tighten, and a climax tears through me—I come like an explosion, legs shaking so violently that my knees threaten to buckle. She chokes a little but doesn't stop, sucking everything down until I am utterly spent.

Her lips pop off. She gazes up at me with such love and adoration it is like a wave crashing over me.

"I love you," I say. "I love you with all my heart—and I tell myself every day how lucky I am to have you."

"It is me who's fortunate to have you," she says. And she means it.

I help her stand and walk her backward to the bed. My legs tremble, and my cock is sticky and spent, but I know the moment I get my hands on my wife's delectable body, the lethargy will fade.

"Sit, sweetheart. Lift your nightgown and spread your naughty legs." Her cheeks turn pink. She is very shy about revealing herself to me, and tonight is no exception.

But I'm a patient man. I unbutton my shirt, watching as she plays with her gown. She pulls the hem to her knees and fidgets with it there, taking it no higher.

I draw my shirt over my shoulders and let it fall to the floor, then kick off my boots and socks, and shuck my pants down. All the while, my eyes are on my pretty wife as I wait for her to do as she has been told.

"Perhaps you don't need my attention," I tease. "Perhaps you are ready to sleep?"

She huffs out a little breath, fingers fidgeting with her gown again in an unconscious tease before she finally tugs it up all the way to her waist.

"That's my good girl. Now open your legs nice and wide. Let me see if you're ready for me."

She spreads her thighs slowly, a faint tremble in her hands where they fist the hem of her nightgown. The scent of arousal hits me, and my softened cock gives an appreciative flex.

I sink to my knees before her. "You are absolutely drenched, sweetheart," I say, sliding my thumb along her inner thigh until I reach the slick treasure between. She whimpers as I press my thumb into the sticky wetness and draw gentle circles.

"Oh, goddess," she mumbles.

"Lie back, sweetheart. You have made quite a mess. Your husband might need to be here for a good while."

She groans and falls back against the bed, throwing one arm across her eyes as though to shield herself from what I'm about to do. I smirk, drag her ass to the edge of the bed, and lower my lips to her sweet pussy.

"Oh, oh!" she cries, one hand fisting the covers beside her.

I lift my head. "Is it too much, sweetheart? Would you like me to stop?"

"No!" It comes out in a strangled squeak.

Chuckling, I go back to my dutiful work, sliding two fingers into her weeping pussy and slowly pumping as I lavish her clit with my tongue. I've barely begun when she's emitting a filthy little groan and gushing all around my finger and over my willing tongue.

She lies panting in the aftermath, and I press a gentle kiss to her inner thigh. My cock is hard. Seeing her find her release has a predictable effect on me. She is simply stunning. I love to pleasure her. It is a gift like no other. I wonder if she wishes to settle down for the night, now. Perhaps she is ready to go to sleep. But then I see her legs twitch before she spreads them wider, invitingly. My fingers are still buried intimately inside her, and I begin to move again... testing.

"Oh," she says, on a dreamy kind of breath.

"Is that nice, sweetheart?"

"Yes."

"Do you need my cock?"

She heaves a ragged breath. "Yes."

"Undo the pretty ribbons on your gown and play with your tits, then."

She fumbles with the little pink ribbons until the material falls away. I finger fuck her, watching as she cups her voluptuous breasts, squeezing them.

"Pinch your nipples," I say.

She shakes her head.

"Clara, if you want me to fuck you, you will do as I say."

She emits a cute little whine even as she does as she is told. She is very needy tonight. Needy in ways I have never known her to be before. As I finger fuck her, and watch my wife toy with her tits, my mind strays to how she looked when she was dancing with Frederick: the flush on her cheeks, her bright eyes. I imagine his fingers here, and her taste lingering on his lips.

I slide a third finger in her, and she arches up off the bed.

"Alex?"

"Hush, sweetheart, you can take this for me." I don't know what has come over me, but I am much enamored with the thought of stretching her out, of forcing her to endure more than she is comfortable with. "Does that feel good?"

"Ye-esss."

"Good girl. Try and relax more for me. That's it."

My thumb circles her clit and, as I work my fingers in and out, the filthy wet noises tell me she is enjoying what I do. I want to do more, to force another finger in, to see just how much she can take.

"Goddess, Alex! I'm going to—"

She comes apart, pussy spasming over my fingers and snapping the last of my control. I crawl over her and capture her cheek in my hand as I close my mouth over hers. She kisses me back, entwining her arms around my neck as our tongues tangle.

She liked that.

I liked that, too.

The little warning bell is going off inside me, but I don't heed it. "I need to take you roughly," I say, tearing my lips from hers. "I want you on your hands and knees."

She blinks up at me, shaking her head. "I... I don't think... It's not proper."

"Anything that takes place between a man and his wife is proper," I say. "If they are both congenial and enjoy it. Do you enjoy it? Do you want me to put my cock in you like that?" She nods helplessly. We are both helpless to the same pull. I strip her of her gown, put her on her hands and knees, and gently press her head into the covers.

"God, you are so beautiful," I say as I come behind her, her full tits hanging down like an offering. It is one I cannot hope to resist. Reaching around, I pinch her nipple. She moans and pushes into my hand for more. It's like a fever has taken hold of me; as if a frenzied, animalistic state of mind is in control.

"It's going to get a little rough," I say, "but you will bear it, won't you, sweetheart?"

"Please," she says, "I will."

She's trembling with her need. Her feminine juices leak from her pussy to glisten over the top of her inner thighs. I pause to run my fingers through the sticky mess before sliding my fingers into her from behind. She twitches and groans, lifting her ass as though seeking more.

I'm in a state of confused arousal, gripped by needs I'm not ready to acknowledge, as I line up and thrust. I'm normally gentler with her, but now I take her hips in my hands and pound into her pussy. She screeches and begs for more, canting her ass even higher to encourage me.

She comes almost immediately, hot pussy fisting my cock. But I'm not done with her.

Not by a long shot. I foresee a long night of carnality ahead.

Chapter Five

Alex

We rise late for breakfast the following day, to find that Frederick's already in the dining room, seated at the table where we enjoyed dinner last night. The patio doors are open, bringing a warm, pleasant breeze into the room.

My sweet wife is blushing as Frederick offers his greeting to us. I lean in and kiss her cheek. "It's not like he could hear what we were doing, sweetheart... Although you *were* very loud," I whisper with a smirk.

"Alex," she hisses, turning away, but not before I see her smile as I hold out a chair for her.

She selects some fruit from the serving plate in the center of the dining table. I elect to pour a coffee instead and forgo a seat.

"Is that all you're having?" Frederick asks, nodding his head at my wife's plate.

"I'm a little unsettled," she admits, and the shy glance she sends my way might as well be an announcement.

Frederick chuckles. "Hmm, so I heard. Well, best keep your strength up."

I nearly choke on my coffee and am forced to thump my chest before I can take a breath. When I glance at her, I find my wife near crimson.

Frederick is smirking as he draws his cup of coffee to his lips. "There is nothing wrong with having an ardent wife. You're a lucky man, Alex."

My eyes twinkle as they shift to my wife. "So I tell myself every day."

It is not often I think about Frederick as an alpha. Not that one can really forget it when one looks at him, for he is everything that designation is known for. And yet he wears the civilized trappings so well.

He artfully changes the subject to the new cottage garden, which my wife is planning. I leave them to their conversation, taking my coffee to the open patio doors where I can gaze out.

The courtyard beyond is sheltered by trees to either side, while directly ahead is an open vista offering views across the meadows. I am taking in the view but also standing somewhere where my erection will not be noted. I shouldn't be aroused by the image that continues to visit my mind: that of my wife with another man. And yet, I cannot dispute that my eagerness last night was in part due to the fantasy I had conjured of the two of them together, imagining the dark interest on Frederick's face as he gazed upon her naked body.

My wife is beautiful, and demure in many ways, and yet there is a wanton underneath.

I imagine his big hands cupping her tits.

26

I take a sip of coffee and fight back a groan. I've lost all sense of propriety. *It is her own fault,* I tell myself with a smile. When a wife greets her husband in such a way, sinks to her knees, and sucks his cock like it is her favorite treat, little wonder I am still lost in a fog of passion.

Our intimate life is very good. I enjoy her body often, love to pleasure her, and am enrapt by the way her face is transfigured when she comes.

Yet, I know there was something a little out of the ordinary in her reactions last night, a wildness I wish to share with her again.

Is it Frederick's influence in some way?

I glance over my shoulder to where they are talking at the dining table, and I'm captivated again by the sight. How tiny she is next to him. The way he leans in, almost protectively, to hear what she has to say. There is nothing improper about anything they do, and yet just the sight of them there continues to stir my improper thoughts.

I shouldn't want my friend to fuck my wife.

It should disgust me.

And yet, I am hard—again—at the mere thought.

Gods, how am I going to get through the day? I enjoyed her often last night and then again this morning before we left the room. I should not have the capacity to get hard, but it's like my cock has a mind of its own, and I can't seem to escape the mental quagmire in which I find myself.

Clara

Alex is looking at me like *that* again. He has taken his coffee to stand beside the open patio doors with his back to us, yet every time he glances back, I can feel the heat in his gaze. I dare not lift my head and meet his eyes when I am holding my own libido back by a mere thread. Between my husband's heated glances and Frederick's deep, rumbling voice, with which he speaks to me in an intimately low tone, forcing me to lean in to hear, I am like a ship adrift in a stormy, carnal sea.

I have never even noticed Frederick's scent before. Today, it's like a rich, potent cloud tickling the back of my throat, and I cannot escape it nor its effect. My nipples are hard, and my pussy is weeping. A little of that is due to my husband's ardor last night and this morning, but I would be lying to myself if I claimed it was all down to that.

"You are not eating much, Clara," Frederick says, in a low voice, close to my ear. "Are you not hungry? You have done no more than move the fruit around your plate. I'm truly sorry if my teasing has made you uncomfortable in some way."

"Oh, no, don't be," I mumble, then make the mistake of glancing sideways at him. And I am caught up in the beauty of his hazel eyes with their long, long lashes. How did I never notice how pretty they were before? How can such a masculine man have such eyes? Surely, there is some unwritten law of creation to protect mortal women from their hypnotic powers. "You have very pretty eyes."

He smirks.

I blink a few times before, mortified, I snatch my gaze back to my plate, where I have, as he indicated, done nothing more than move the fruit around.

Why would I say that?

What madness has gotten into me?

I throw a nervous glance across at my husband, to find him staring at me.

Did he hear me? Does he see the condition I am in, aroused and needy while I think about his friend thrusting his coffee aside, spreading me out on the table, and sliding one of the plump strawberries through my slick pussy before presenting it to my lips, with a smirk? *"There, does that taste better now?"* the fantasy version of Frederick purrs.

I swallow.

"Clara, if I might have a word," Alex says.

Chapter Six

Alex

I take her hand to usher her from the table. "Excuse us for a moment, Frederick."

"Of course," he says, rising to his feet as she stands. On resuming his seat, he reaches for his coffee then leans back in his chair.

I escort my wife out through the patio doors and across the sun-warmed flagstones to the side of the sheltered space. There, before I have even thought through my intentions, I have her caught in my arms, my hips pinning hers against the handy stone balustrade that surrounds the patio "I need you," I say, bluntly, looking down into her eyes

"Oh! Alex!" Her eyes are perfectly round as she stares up at me. "What are you doing?"

"Bend over, love."

I steal a kiss as she gasps, and then I spin her around. I run my hands over her hips and then up along either side of her spine to gently push her shoulders and then her head down. How did I never notice this was the perfect height?

"Frederick," she hisses. "He might see us."

"He won't," I say, more confidently than I feel. I don't care if he does see us.

I have a hand on her skirts, about to lift them, when I pause at the thought—Do I want him to see us?

Perhaps. I don't know anything except that I am possessed with desire for Clara.

"I need you," I repeat.

"Oh, gods," she says, a faint whine in her voice, but she doesn't try to stop me when I lift up her skirt.

I groan to myself when I see she's not wearing any panties. "Did you forget something, wife?"

"I'm so sorry," she says, her voice muffled where I have tossed her long skirts over her head. "I put some on, and then.... Well, they were saturated. So I took them off and then... I was going to get some clean ones, and the next thing you were ushering me downstairs announcing we were late!"

"Good," I say decisively, my hands filled with the plump globes of her ample ass. "I like you without them. From now on, you shall not wear them again. It will be our little secret."

My hand is on my buckle, and then I'm shucking my pants down in a daze. My cock is hot and heavy in my hand as I line up and thrust into my wife's drenched pussy. I fucked her many times last night and again this morning, so it's little wonder she is ready for me.

I pump my hips, pounding into her, making our flesh slap together and her ass jiggle with every thrust. Fuck, I'm never going to last.

She moans lowly. "Oh gods—humph—Oh gods!" Her voice is breathy, and her words stuttered between my thrusts. "What if—huff—somebody sees?"

Somebody? She means Frederick, and just thinking about him seeing us like this is near enough to send me over the edge. "They won't." I interject confidence. "Be a good girl for me and let me fuck you how I need."

"What if...oh!"

"Keep quiet, sweetheart," I say. "Lest we stir Frederick's curiosity."

She moans loudly.

"Clara, put your fingers in your mouth if you need to."

I hear her moan around them, while I'm busy enjoying the view of her jiggling ass and the sounds of our flesh slapping together, the way she flutters around my cock, and how deliciously wet she is. Gods, why have I never done this before?

"Mun...mrmmmn...umhfff."

I believe she is complaining around her fingers at the vigor of my strokes. I know that if it were something serious, she would take them out, and so I only grin at her huffs and grunts.

"I am the master of this home, am I not? You are my wife. If I want to fuck you, I shall."

I have never spoken so boldly to Clara before this, but her enthusiastic groan and the sticky squelching noises her pussy begins to make tell me she is not averse to my possessive demands.

"It is for the best you don't have any panties on," I say, my eyes are on the place where I shuttle in and out of her, watching my cock disappear, glistening with her arousal. "When I come inside you, they will only get soaked again."

She moans again.

I reach forward and run my hands over the fabric covering her plump tits before I rip her bodice down so I can cup them and pinch her nipples as I fuck her.

She moans louder around her fingers, her body swaying as I fuck her roughly against the stone balustrade. The coarse surface is probably doing terrible things to her dress, but I can't seem to care. The only clear thought in my mind is that Clara is as enthusiastic about this as I am.

"Come for me, sweetheart. Come all over my cock like a good wife should."

Her pussy clamps over my length as she emits a filthy moan, loud enough for me to be certain she has forgotten to keep her fingers in her mouth. My balls rise. My spine tingles and my mind blanks out as I shoot cum against the entrance of her womb. And, all the while, she moans and thrusts her ass back for more, crushing my dick in a series of spasms as she comes around me.

I slow my thrusts, then release her tits so that I can pull her hips tight against me as I pump into her a few last times. She shudders. We are both breathing heavily. I don't look back to check whether Frederick came to see what we are doing. I tell myself I hope he didn't. And yet... I really wish he did.

I ease out of her. A thick blob of cum drops and splats against the flagstones.

"Oh gods," she says, struggling to rise.

"Wait there, my love," I say, "and I shall help you up." I don't move to do so yet, however, for the view is compelling —her tits are out, her plump ass is on display, and her pussy is dripping cum all over the flagstones. I take my time putting myself away.

"Let me help you with your gown first," I say. I'm quite slow about this, as I enjoy playing with her body. Cupping her ass cheeks and gently pulling them apart and then squeezing them back together and watching another blob of cum drip out.

"Oh!" she gasps, as another quiver runs through her body. "Alex, what are you doing?!"

Somehow, I gain command of myself enough to lower her skirts and help her up, turning her around to face me.

My cock jerks. I am spent, and yet it jerks again at the image of her breasts spilling lewdly from the bodice of her gown. She has such glorious fat tits, with nipples that are big and so sensitive to the touch. I am a man under a spell and I cannot help but lean forward and draw one rosy tip into my mouth.

My groan as I suck on her heated flesh is one of pure sensual pleasure. It's all I can do not to toss up her skirts and bend her over the damn balustrade again.

My lips pop off with a sigh of regret.

I help her straighten her gown, and she huffs a little as she tries to set her bodice to rights. Her hair is a wild mess, her cheeks flushed, and her eyes bright.

I purse my lips, asking for divine guidance as I see how swollen her tits are from my mauling, threatening to spill back out.

"I think I need to go to my room and find a different dress," she mutters, with a tiny sob.

"It'll be fine, sweetheart," I say, drawing her against me, unable to help myself from running my fingertips over the swell of her breast. "You look perfectly decent."

She's not decent by a long shot. From my taller vantage point, I can see the distinct upper edge of her areola above the decolletage of her gown. If she breathes too heavily, I swear her nipple will pop out.

I believe it makes me the wickedest of husbands that I like her being in this state. "Here, let me help you with your hair."

She is distracted from adjusting her bodice any further,

as is my intent, when I delve my fingers into her tresses in what is a vain attempt to detangle her hair.

"Oh, it's all knotty!"

"Only a little," I say. Her hair is the least of her concerns when she looks so thoroughly ravished. "I doubt Frederick will notice, and even if he should, he would never mention it. You know he's a very civilized man, and one might almost forget he was an alpha."

Her smile is one of relief. "He is, isn't he? I was so sad about what happened with Rebecca."

I lean down and kiss her sweet lips. "I know, my love, as were we all. But Rebecca is happy now. Her centaur mate is a little rough around the edges, to be sure, but they have found their way with each other."

"I just hate to think of Frederick all on his own. He doesn't seem to want anyone else."

"Trust me, he does not want for female attention," I say dryly.

She blushes anew and won't meet my gaze as she mutters, "Well, I'm sure he does not!"

"Come, I'm going to get you that cup of coffee you missed out on."

When we return to the dining room it is empty, and the double doors leading to the sitting room are open. "There, Frederick was not even in the room." Regardless of my words, I am struck with a certainty that he heard what we did. Maybe he lingered in the open patio door before he left the room... Or perhaps I am altogether wrong, and he left immediately when we went outside and knows nothing of what transpired. There is no denying the twinge of disappointment I feel at that last thought

I glance over Clara's shoulder, into the sitting room, and I see Frederick through the open doors. He raises both brows, smirks at me, and slowly shakes his head before lifting his coffee in salute and bringing it to his lips.

The sudden thrill that races through me whites out my mind and creates a tornado, low in my belly.

He knows what we just did.

"Maybe I should return to our room and straighten myself out?"

Hell, no. Now that I have ventured down this dark path, nothing can pull me back. "Nonsense. Let me get you a fresh cup of coffee. And then you can keep Frederick company." It would be the gentlemanly thing to do to escort her back to our room. Only, as I have discovered today, there is no gentleman in me where this is concerned.

"I would be delighted in your company, Clara," he calls from the other room as I go to the sideboard to pour the coffee for her

"Of course." She turns to smile at Frederick. When I return to her side, Clara glances back up at me, missing the heat in Frederick's deeply admiring gaze as it sweeps over her.

The hungry look is gone as quickly as it appeared, and by the time she turns back to him, the suave mask has returned to his face.

Gods, I cannot breathe. I need a moment to compose myself. "I have some business to attend to." I offer my wife an encouraging smile when she pouts prettily. "I won't be long."

With a chaste kiss on her forehead, I slip out of the room.

As the door clicks shut behind me, I plant my back against it and suck in a sharp, ragged breath.

What the hell am I doing? I just fucked my wife in front

of my best friend. It's like I'm throwing her at him and can't seem to make myself stop.

He's still an alpha, and I need to remember that. I'm teetering upon a dangerous edge, only I want to plummet—I want to tumble headfirst deep down into the dark, sensual abyss.

But, most of all, I want my best friend to fuck my wife.

Chapter Seven

Frederick

I would have to be deaf and stupid not to know what they were about.

I think I suspected something even before I heard her little whimpers carried on the breeze. And then Alex simply brings her back into the room, thoroughly rumpled from whatever the fuck he has just done to pleasure her in some way. Did he put her on her knees first and coach her to suck him off? Did he lift her pretty skirt and eat her out?

As she draws closer, though, I can tell exactly what they did. I can smell him all over her. It is both a blessing and a curse to be an alpha. Betas can be mistaken in thinking little beyond the fact that we are bigger and stronger, and overlook the fact that we have an outstanding sense of smell... and filthy fucking minds.

When a man takes a woman outside in the urgent manner Alex just did, 'having words' is not the first thing that comes to my mind.

I sip my coffee to hide my smirk as the ravished version of Clara is left alone with a wolf.

She takes a seat beside me in the manner of a woman whose legs are about to give out and looks anywhere but at me.

I don't know what is going on between them, but they are ravenous for one another.

Good for him. He's a lucky bastard, and I've told him as much many times. His wife is gorgeous, with the kind of hips and ass that could make even a level-headed man think with his dick. I can't even think about her tits without my cock wanting to fucking go off. Then there is her air of sweet innocence that belies the charms of her body and her easy acquiescence to what her dear husband just did.

The cup shakes against the saucer in her hands.

"Here." I take it off her and set it down on the side table. I clear my throat and try to think of something, anything, I might say to break the tension that invades the small space between us.

"Are you well, Clara?"

Why the fuck did I just open that door?

"No!" It comes out in a squeak.

I chuckle, but catching her stricken look, I get both my inner beast and amusement under control. "I'm sorry. I don't mean to laugh at your discomfort. It's more that you're cursed to look adorable no matter how thoroughly loved your husband leaves you."

She throws a glance my way. I meet and hold it for all of a second before my eyes lower to her fucking tits. Gods, they are a test. The way that the bodice of her dress is drooping, I can distinctly see the top of her dark areolae. Now I am staring at her fucking tits, and I cannot fucking stop.

"Your dress might need a little... adjustment." I swallow, and finally drag my gaze away.

"Oh." It comes out all breathy and floods my mind with filthy thoughts as she battles to right her gown.

I haven't thumped Alex since we were children, before I revealed as an alpha, but I'm thinking about thumping him right now. What the fuck is wrong with him? He should have escorted her to their bedroom, where she might have tended to this privately.

The man may be one of my oldest friends, but he is assuredly acting like an idiot today.

A small sob escapes her lips.

"Clara?" I make the mistake of glancing back. I don't know what the fuck she's done, but her tit is now red and blotchy, and one nipple is fully out. I don't breathe for the longest period of time as she fumbles with her gown, trying to tug the decolletage up even as she attempts to squash her plump tit down.

It is a battle doomed to failure.

"You are swollen with arousal." The words escape my lips without the permission of my brain.

"Oh, goddess," she whimpers. The distress in her voice is palpable, and it finally cools my lust enough that I can drag my gaze away from her fat nipple to her flushed face and desperate eyes.

"Hush, Clara. Let me help you with that."

Her hands fall away, leaving her tits quivering with her every shuddering breath.

I'm in a trance as I lean toward her. My head moves down. My mouth is fucking watering even before I get a taste. She emits a needy little moan that reaches straight to my core as I close my lips around the distended peak and suck. I suck again, pulling the tight little nub deeper into my mouth.

A low, rumbly purr escapes me with my next breath. I open my mouth wider, and this time I draw a generous portion of her tit into my mouth along with her nipple. I exhale heavily, feasting greedily on her hot, delectable flesh, feeling instantly calmed by the act of suckling on her. Gods, I could feast here all day. How the fuck Alex ever lets her out of their bedroom is a mystery to me.

She tastes delightful.

She smells amazing.

There's nothing sweeter than a lusty female. Her scent and helpless moans pull a thread straight through my gut and down into my balls. My cock flexes against my pants. I am much enamored with this needy female, and I don't even care that she is my best friend's wife.

Her fingers find my hair: not to pull me off. No, they hold me there.

I shift, nuzzling her soft flesh, getting lost in the fog. Somehow, I manage to lift my head. My chest feels tight, like there's not enough air in the room, as we stare into each other's eyes.

I have stepped over a line.

Her hands slip from my hair. Her tit is now half out and considerably more exposed than before. I believe I have not helped her with the problem at all. I believe I have made matters worse.

"Here," I say, "let us loosen the little bow. I believe it will help."

I undo the top ribbon, and it puts slack into her pretty jade-green dress. When I gently tug her gown, her decolletage covers her, although I'm disgusted with myself for even thinking to cover it up. If I had my way, her tits would spend most of the day on display, awaiting my pleasure, encouraging me to *play*.

But now the ribbon is open, and her breasts make an arresting V as they quiver beautifully under her ragged breaths.

"There." It is not entirely decent, but it is not indecent either.

"Th-thank you," she stammers, her eyes down.

It is then that her husband chooses to return. The door clicks shut behind him. We both turn to look at him. I don't know if I look guilty. Clara certainly does. As I lean back into my chair, his eyes shift between us. He doesn't look like he's about to go at me or kick me out of his house.

He looks interested.

He looks like a man about to ravish his wife again.

I swear, if the bastard drags her somewhere to fuck her again and leaves me hanging on his pleasure, I will thump him, whether he is my best friend or not.

Only, I wonder what might be the consequence if I choose to meet the matter head-on?

"You left your poor wife in some discomfort," I say. "Did you just fuck her on the veranda?"

She gasps. I don't pay her any mind, aware that I've ventured onto dangerous ground, yet I cannot pull fucking back.

"Over the balustrade," Alex admits.

I chuckle. "Where anyone could see. Where *I* could see."

"Did you?" he asks, and there is no mistaking the eagerness in his tone nor the way his face lights with interest.

His sweet wife doesn't say a word, but I can feel her quivering next to me. I hear the unsteady saw of her breathing.

I shake my head. "No. I did what a civilized man would do. I pretended that nothing was going on." I turn to Clara, and her pretty blue eyes slam into mine. I could sink into them. She is so beautiful. Sweet-natured. Her biggest fault is that she believes the best of people. Unfortunately, the world is cruel, and some people are bastards who don't deserve her charm. But it is hard to fault someone for being too kind, for being too gullible. Alex tries to protect her from the world, and I admire him for that.

Except, now, he's thrusting his sweet wife in front of an alpha. Sometimes, he forgets what I am, that an alpha has an inner beast, that his senses are sharper, and that we have deep, barbaric lusts.

And that, on occasion, our pheromones can have an influence over betas.

None of that has happened with Clara and Alex before, and they have ever been my friends. Oh, I've noticed Clara, for certain—I'd have to be fucking blind not to. However, I am not the kind of bastard who would act on it, ever, and doubly not when it is obvious to anyone that there is a deep love between them.

But, this time, something has changed, and it is not all down to me.

My hand shakes a little as I dare to run my knuckles down her soft cheek, waiting for a reaction from Alex while wondering what I'll do if he tells me to fuck off. He doesn't. "Did he come inside you, Clara?"

She nods slowly, her lips parted as she pants a little. Her eyes are glazed, pupils blown and fixed on mine. They are both getting off on my scent. So what should I do about it?

I should leave. That would be the right thing, the sensible thing, and in a day or two, maybe as much as a week, the influence would start to wear off, and they would come out of the spell, doubtless embarrassed about what they had done.

Except I'm fucking lonely for a connection beyond the quick fucks I indulge in with practiced betas and the occasional mated omega who needs another dick when in heat. Visiting Alex and Clara has become a highlight for me over recent years. I never really asked myself why. Now, I begin to wonder about it at a deeper level. Have I always coveted my friend's wife?

I had thought I wanted her sister, Rebecca. In some ways, I did. Circumstances and their bitchy older sister destroyed any chance of that. I spent a year searching for Rebecca. When I found her, I knew she was already lost to me. I offered her the protection of my name when I realized she was with child, even as I understood it would be my name only, for her heart was claimed.

I was trying to do the right thing by her, to give her an option when it appeared she had none. Nothing I offered was done with the intention of poaching another male's woman, and I was genuinely glad when they both came to their senses and committed to one another.

So, I have never coveted a mated or married woman before, although many couples have sought my attention, to see if I was amenable to fulfilling a fantasy or desire—to be an extra dick. And I have engaged in that sort of play, more often than not, because I'm a man with a healthy appetite where fucking is concerned, and the experience was universally hot.

But I never wanted more, even though I enjoyed the experience.

It is different with Alex, perhaps because we have been friends since we were children, or perhaps I have always secretly coveted his wife. Can I go down this road? Can I give them what they both so clearly desire, a hot fantasy, and then walk away?

I only know that I can't walk away *yet*.

I rest my hand on the back of her neck and gently work my thumb along the column.

Alex swallows; his eyes are on my fingers—he doesn't tell me to stop. I've been in this situation enough times to read the signs. When I glance down at his crotch, his cock jerks against his pants.

So, this is how it is going to play out, is it?

He's not a mere acquaintance, and I already know this won't be an encounter I can forget. What happens will change things between us, irrevocably.

I realize all these things, and I don't care.

This will all be on their terms, as it always is. Only, this time, it could end badly. He might rescind his permission at any point. Maybe he just likes the thought and not the reality of an alpha fucking his beta wife. Maybe he will take her out on the balcony again and fuck her, and I will be left hanging.

Maybe he will take her loudly and enthusiastically tonight while I lie in my own bed with my cock in my hand, imagining what they do.

Maybe he will let me watch them.

Maybe he will send me packing.

Or maybe he won't.

It's a risk I'm prepared to take.

Chapter Eight

Clara

Frederick's hand is at the back of my neck. It is a big, rough hand. It circles nearly all the way around. His thumb slides up and down at the side of my throat, absently.

Breathing is a challenge as the air whispers in and out of my lungs. My husband is staring at me... no, not me *per se*, but at the place where Frederick touches me. He licks his lips. He doesn't mind how his friend handles me. He really doesn't.

I want to ask questions, yet the words cannot form.

We have crossed boundaries. We have crossed them in a way from which there is no going back. I love my husband with all my heart. I have never once coveted the attention of another man. I barely look at them, truth be told. It's like they don't really exist in that way—even Frederick has been in this category before now. I have looked at him more as an opportunity to match-make my unmated, unwedded friends, constructing happily-ever-afters where they have lavish weddings and children and where we are lifelong friends.

I always liked these scenarios because I couldn't bear the thought of Frederick marrying somebody who was horrible. *Mating*, I correct myself, for alphas do not wed.

There is something strange in the way my husband watches his friend touching me, a sort of intense focus, one I feel echoes inside me.

I feel a confession bubbling up, the need to explain what just happened while Alex was out of the room. My nipple still throbs where Frederick sucked—it's like he's still sucking me there.

Only how can I get the words out? I feel ashamed to my very core, but also hot and needy, like I might die if Frederick were to take his hand away.

Belatedly, I realize they've been talking for some time and, further, talking about me.

"...so it's a different approach one must take with a beta than with an omega?"

I catch up with the end of my husband's question.

"It is," Frederick confirms.

He removes his hand from the back of my neck, and I miss it instantly. But his fingertips settle again at my shoulder, and then they glide over my collarbone and all the way over the swell of my breast. They pause at the next bow on my bodice, and he gives a gentle tug.

My bodice gives. His fingertips skim along the edges of the gaping material as my breathing turns erratic and shallow.

Alex doesn't tell him to stop. I feel he ought to.

I feel I ought to move or slap Frederick for his presumptuousness, only I don't. That ship has sailed, so to speak. I've already had his mouth on me, felt the sweet, insistent pull of his lips, suckling me.

For a moment, my mind goes blank to everything but that memory. I'm shuddering with arousal, and all he's doing is playing with the upper swell of my breast—little swirling patterns with the tips of his rough fingers.

"You need more preparation?" Alex asks. His voice sounds a little strained, maybe, but it's hard to be certain with confidence over the whooshing of blood pounding through my veins.

Frederick tugs at my decolletage, and my breast pops out. I squeak a protest even though I don't move to stop him as his big hand cups the weight. Then he squeezes my taut nipple between his finger and thumb, and I squirm in my seat, face flaming to a heat.

"For certain. An alpha can't just fuck a beta."

Goddess, those blunt words. Alex rarely swears in my presence. Whenever he does, it makes me feel a little hot and naughty. Given that I am already on fire at Frederick's treatment of me, his words make me whimper with need.

"And what would one do then?" Alex asks, all interest, as his best friend, an alpha, plays with my nipple, squeezing it, tugging it, rolling it only just on the side of too rough. I try to steady my breathing and not to squirm.

"Some alphas even prefer betas," Frederick says.

"They do?" Alex asks, tearing his eyes from my breast to meet Frederick's gaze.

"Hmm. A man can get a little lust drunk with an omega. One male is not always enough, and you must share. I cannot imagine ever sharing a woman with another alpha; I always knew I was too dominant for such an approach. There was a time when I thought I wanted an omega.

While I'm not a deeply philosophical man, perhaps things happen for a reason."

He is talking about Rebecca, but it's hard to hold onto the words when he is toying with me. His hand trails across to the other side, and I gasp as he bestows attention on the neglected nipple.

"She's more sensitive here."

"She is," my husband agrees.

"So, yes, there will need to be some preparation, which might take anything from a number of hours to a number of days, or even longer. It can be a challenge even without the knot."

I shudder.

He pinches my nipple and just holds it.

I can't breathe properly, and I begin to squirm.

"Try and sit still, love," The endearment rolls off Frederick's tongue, and it freezes me in place.

My frantic gaze shifts to my husband. His throat bobs as he swallows.

"Some betas respond better than others," Frederick continues. "And are naturally more compatible with an alpha; and the connection increases further over time. There is not so large a difference between a beta who has been bonded to an alpha for a number of years and an omega. Some venture to make nests, much to their alpha's delight. When they are fertile, it can have an almost rut-like effect on their mates."

He withdraws his fingers. My breathing is choppy, and my nipple throbs.

My pussy is drenched and likewise throbs.

He turns toward me and brushes his knuckles absently back and forth over the swell at the side of my breast.

"Your wife has beautiful tits. I don't think I really appreciated them before. Always closeted away behind her... dress. Imagine how full these will be when she is with child. I can well imagine that a naughty wife like Clara would seek her husband's lips to ease the pressure when the little one is full."

My pussy clenches savagely.

He returns his fingers to my nipple, seizes it and tugs vigorously, and my whole body locks up as pleasure tears through me.

Oh my god, oh my god, oh my god, oh my god, oh my god! I come, panting, gasping, my pussy clenching over nothing, shocked by this turn of events.

"There," Frederick says, finally releasing my poor abused nipple. "I think we have established that Clara is one such woman who takes well to an alpha."

I sit there, panting and confused, staring at my hands resting on my lap and so hot I fear I might catch fire.

"Of course, some try to fake it. Most alphas are wealthy. They want your wealth but don't care much beyond that. A canny alpha knows. See how she's flushed all the way to the upper swell of her tits." He traces his fingers with his words. "Such a reaction cannot be faked. Clara truly is the preferred kind of beta. The kind that responds. It would take only a small amount of preparation for her to take my cock. It would take considerably more work before the knot. You are a very lucky man to have such a sweet and lusty wife who is so very responsive."

"I would like to see you with her."

"Husband!" The word is punched from my lungs, while at the same time my pussy releases another flood of arousal.

"Hush, Clara." Frederick settles his hand on the back of my neck again. "We have already established that you are a little woozy from my pheromones. You couldn't even be trusted to make a sound decision at this point. If I were to take my cock out, you'd be trying to stuff it into your sweet mouth." He traces my lips as if daring me to dispute this. I find I must fight the urge to open and suck the digit into my mouth. "You would not even care that your husband is watching; that he can see what you do."

A whimper escapes me. I don't think any of us is sound of mind at this point.

My husband has just offered me to another man, and I think that surely we are all very much doomed.

Chapter Nine

Frederick

Alex has made the offer, and there is no going back. His sweet wife has just come apart, and all I have done is toy with her nipples.

Gods, she is a wonder. Sweet and yet with perfectly filthy needs. I envy him that he has all this.

Except, I now wonder: what am I? A fancy? Simply part of a little game that they choose to play for the next day or two and then no more? I don't know what I am: besides being an alpha, and dominant. Until the point where he tells me to fuck off, I'm going to let that side of me out.

I close my arm around her waist and pluck her from where she sits, putting her onto my lap.

"Oh! What?" She squeaks and frets a little. But I keep my arm tightly clamped around her waist, enjoying her small struggle and the way her beautiful tits jiggle around.

I lick my lips. Gods, I could play with them all fucking day... and I probably will. I don't know how much time I have with her, but I'm going to enjoy all of it.

Cupping her chin, I turn her to face me, and I brush my thumb over her lower lip. Her eyes are round and a little glazed. "Is it not more comfortable to be sitting on my lap?"

She nods slowly.

"Give me words, love."

"Yes," she breathes.

"Good girl. I want you to enjoy what we do, even if it is a little uncomfortable at times. And it will please me greatly to have your trust. You like to please, don't you, Clara? You like to be a good girl."

Her breathing quickens as she gazes up at me. "Yes."

"I thought so. Now, rest your head against my chest while your husband and I talk."

I kiss the top of her head as she settles, drawing her sweet, aroused scent into my lungs. I keep my hands neutral, letting her get used to the feel of me. Her pretty tits are still out, so she is already becoming accustomed to having her body exposed.

When I glance up, I find Alex staring at us, enrapt.

"How does it feel to see my hands on her?"

"Good," he admits. "It looks really good. She is so... tiny next to you. So precious. Is she not the most beautiful woman you have ever seen?"

"She is," I agree. Distantly, I'm aware that I'm treading a dangerous path. Alphas can imprint upon a beta with the same vigor they imprint on an omega. I must be wary of that. And yet she is utterly adorable, nestled on my lap, with her small weight and her light feminine scent.

"These tits are a test," I say, weakly. Going against my decision to simply hold her, I reach to cup one, enjoying the heavy, comforting weight in my hand.

Alex chuckles softly, "Gods, don't I know? I was

obsessed with them while we were courting. I swear, I jacked off daily to the thought of her quivering tits."

Her gasp is scandalized.

"Surely you're not shocked by your husband's ways? It is ever a test when a man is courting a woman but cannot yet touch her, but he thinks often about doing as much." I turn to Alex. "And she takes well to rutting?"

"She does," he says. Pride fills his voice as he speaks about something that would otherwise be forbidden. "Last night, she even initiated things."

"What did she do?" I ask, my interest piqued.

"Don't—"

I pause my fondling of her tit, concerned that she wants to put a stop to things. Except it is not me Clara is looking at, it is her husband. "There should be no secrets between us," I say. "Not when you've just come so prettily by my hand. I think I have the right to know what you did to your husband and how it pleased him." I resume my play, waiting to see if he'll tell me what she did.

"Gods, it pleased me," Alex says gruffly. "She has an entire collection of scandalous nightgowns with fabric so sheer they might as well be transparent. She dropped to her knees, worked my pants down, and sucked my cock."

"Does she swallow or spit?"

She emits a little whimper, turning her cheek against me as if seeking to hide.

"Swallowed every last drop."

"Such a good girl," I say. "Would it bother you if we shared a kiss?"

Alex shakes his head. "No. I don't think it would."

I close my fingers over her hair and tip her head back. Her lips part as I lower my head and slant my mouth over hers. I swallow her small gasp, still tugging lazily on her nipple as my tongue plunders her mouth. She opens sweetly, but I don't linger.

"How did that feel?" I ask Alex.

"I liked it," he says. "I liked it a lot. It wasn't a lie when I said I wanted you to fuck her."

I smirk. "And how do you feel about *that*, Clara?"

She looks at me seriously, before answering. "I never thought about it before, but now I'm struggling to think about anything else." She turns to her husband. "Alex, I love you. I never needed more."

"It arouses me, sweetheart," he says. "When I fucked you last night, I was thinking about you with Frederick. I love you so much. But I love that he wants you, too. It makes me feel proud that I have such a stunning, desirable wife. One who is enthusiastic in matters of lust. One who lets me bend her over a stone balustrade and take her. It pleases me greatly that someone else admires you the way I do."

I believe Clara is shocked at the bluntness with which he speaks. Her mouth opens as if she has something to say, but she cannot muster any words. Her lips are irresistible, and I tip her head again and kiss her. This time, I let a little more of my dominance out, plundering her mouth as I play roughly with her nipple, swallowing her moan as she arches against me.

When I lift my lips, we are all breathing heavily, and it takes great strength of will to tuck her head down against my chest and withdraw my hand from her tit.

"We should speak plainly," I say to Alex. "Exactly what are your terms?"

"I don't want to place boundaries," he says. "I've seen you kiss and handle her. It only arouses me."

"And if I kiss her here?" I ask, stroking light circles around the areola of her nipple. She doesn't fidget this time; but lets me do what I please.

"I would not mind."

"And her cunt. You would let me fuck her cunt?"

"Yes," he says raggedly, his eyes turning glazed. "Yes, I would."

"You could let me push my fat alpha cock into her tight beta pussy?"

"Yes," he says, "yes, I could."

"And what about her ass? Have you taken her there?"

She fidgets at that. I squeeze and hold her nipple, and she huffs out a little breath.

"Settle yourself, love. We're discussing what you need."

Her chest heaves, but then she relaxes, and I release her nipple. It is fat and flushed with arousal. I smirk as she pushes her chest into my hand as though seeking more. She's definitely taking well to my ways, which is for the best.

"Only with my finger," Alex says thickly, rousing me from my study of his wife. "We were trying to build up to it, but she's very nervous, and we don't get very far."

"You use oil?"

He nods. "Have some on the nightstand that's natural for a body. She likes the touch. She's just a little conflicted and nervous about it."

"You haven't fucked her there then?"

He shakes his head.

"And do you want to?"

"Damn right, I want to."

"Good. We shall see if we can work her up to that."

She goes to stammer a protest, but I tip her chin. "Do

you have something to say on this, Clara? Do you or do you not like it when your husband puts his fingers in your ass?"

"I like it, but..."

"There is no but, you either like it or you don't."

"I don't like it."

Alex makes a scoffing noise.

"Are you lying to me, Clara?" My voice deepens, and my eyes narrow.

She gulps.

"It is a very bad idea to lie to an alpha, especially something as important as how we fuck you."

She shakes her head, mouth opening and closing, her eyes searching mine.

"Were you lying to me, Clara? You just changed the story halfway through."

"I'm... I'm nervous."

"That was not the question I asked you. I asked you if you liked it. And if the next thing that comes out of your mouth is anything but a yes or no, you'll be going straight over my lap, and your bottom will be spanked. So, think very carefully before you say the next words. Did you like it when your husband put his fingers inside your bottom? Did you like it when he thrust it in and out? Did it feel a tingly kind of good?"

"Yes." She nods hopelessly, her eyes darting to her husband.

"Good girl. I'm so pleased with you for telling us the truth. Know that we shall definitely be touching you there. Your husband wants to watch me fuck you. Are you agreeable to that? Do you want to be rutted by an alpha? Do you like the thought of that?"

She nods again.

"The words, love. Tell me the words."

"Yes, Frederick, I do."

My nostrils flare as her submission sends blood pounding into my cock. "Now, just as your husband likes the thought of me fucking you, I very much like the thought of him fucking your virgin ass while I watch. Ass fucking is delicious, filthy, and darkly depraved. I think a woman like you, who is enthusiastic in matters of lust, would take well to it. I think you will come hard and fast when your husband enjoys you there. I think you will do all manner of depraved things with a little coaching."

Her eyes search mine and she bites her bottom lip as a little shiver runs through her body. "I think I might, too. Oh! I want to come again," she pleads.

"Not yet." I tuck her head back down. Alex now wears a strained expression and is squeezing his cock through his pants.

I grin.

"I nearly fucking came," he says.

"Good. That means we are all congenial to moving forward. That I may fuck your wife while you watch. That you wish very much to take her ass. That she is a little nervous, and that is to be expected. What about me tasting her? What about me eating out her cunt? How do you feel about that?"

"Gods, I definitely want you to," he says. "I think you would enjoy her well."

"I think I would, too. And her lips on my cock? I know you think me civilized, but make no mistake, I am an alpha at my core."

"I want that too."

I look down at Clara.

"Yes," she whispers, burrowing into my chest. "It comes

as a surprise to me when I never considered this before. But, yes, now, I want all of it."

I tip her head up and kiss her temple. She is a delight, so tiny and precious as she nestles on my lap. Yet there is no mistaking the way her thighs rub together as she tries to ease the growing ache.

It's time.

Chapter Ten

Alex

I don't remember how we got to the bedroom, only that we are here. I'm in some kind of trance. I can't quite believe this is happening. An out-of-body experience, if you will, that people sometimes talk about when they are close to death.

Only I don't feel close to death. I feel more alive than I've ever been as I take a seat on a chair placed for my viewing pleasure. He wants to watch me take her ass, an act she has been reluctant about. One I have secretly craved. One I believe Clara will be enthusiastic for by the time Frederick is done with her.

Her hand is in his as they come to a stop at the foot of the bed. She looks small and fragile beside him. He leans in towards her protectively, his focus on her at all times.

I had heard this about alphas and how they are able to sense things below the surface that betas cannot. In the way some animals are able to home and find water, alphas can sense things regarding lust.

"I'm a little nervous," she admits.

He draws her small hand to his lips. "We shall take good care of you, ensure you are thoroughly prepared," he says.

"How will you..." —she swallows— "How will you prepare me?"

He brushes her hair over her shoulder before his fingers find the ribbon at her bodice, the one she foolishly insisted on tying for the short walk to our bedroom. "We will take our time. I will know when you are ready. There will be no fear, only a pleasurable experience."

She gazes up at him, so trusting.

I think it will be more than pleasurable. I think it will be incredible. I also think it will be a terrible strain for her to take his cock.

My throat works as I swallow. I'm asking a man to ruin my wife, to defile her pussy with his thick cock. I don't know why I should like the thought of that, of her being all open when he is done with her. The thought of taking her after him should disgust me, shouldn't it?

It doesn't. It enlivens me. I feel sensitive all across the surface of my skin, and as I brush my knuckles over my lips, even that small sensation is magnified.

He kisses her, gentle nibbles upon her lips that grow in urgency as he divests her of her dress. She hardly notices what he's doing, so caught up in the kiss. It's almost like she's forgotten I am here. I feel a brief stirring of something. I don't quite know what it is. It's not jealousy. But it is a kind of longing. I could stop them. He has already indicated that we should speak plainly if it becomes too much, and I trust him in this even as I understand I'm gifting my wife to a man with an animalistic side, a man with a knot.

As her gown slips to the floor and her naked beauty is revealed, his lips break from hers.

"Gods, you are stunning. I want to shred every gown in your closet and keep you like this all the time. Some alphas do that, you know. Expect their mates to be naked the moment they enter the privacy of their home. Some have the most scandalous kind of clothing they insist their mates wear, little more than pretty wrappers that serve no hindrance to an alpha's frequent desire for rutting."

A thrill passes through me at his words, both his praise and the kind of depraved things an alpha demands of his mate. He echoes all I feel... all I secretly desire. I wish that I could keep her in those naughty undergarments she some-times wears.

He cups her tits together and squeezes them, brushing his thumbs over her nipples before he slides his hands down to her hips. He lifts her and drops her on the bed. "Spread your legs, Clara. Nice and wide. I want to watch you while I undress."

She does so, slowly, demure, her pretty face flushed.

"Tell me how she looks," I ask, unable to mask my eagerness.

He undoes the buttons on his shirt, working down. "She is like the goddess in living flesh. In all my life, I have never seen such beauty. She is perfect. Gods, she is so perfect with her full tits and slick pussy glistening with her need." As he reaches the bottom of his shirt, he tugs it free and tosses it to the floor.

He is a beautiful man, broad-chested and powerful, the definition of alpha masculinity. When he wears clothing, one might almost forget that he is an alpha—and primal—yet there is no disguising any of that as he strips down the rest of his clothing and stands before her naked.

Her chest saws unsteadily, as does mine.

His cock is thick and long. I can already see the faint

swelling near the base—his knot. He takes that monstrosity in his hand and strokes it once, ejecting a long, thin trail of pre-cum that stretches to the bedroom floor before it finally breaks.

Her lips part on a little gasp. My mind splinters between now and last night when I sought to work four fingers into her. It will be a strain for her to take him. I still want him to. The thought of him pushing into her, forcing her flesh to yield, has my cock thumping and leaking behind my pants.

It is suddenly hot in here. I reach for the buttons of my shirt and tug it off impatiently, then I toss it to the floor.

"I'm just going to test you," he says to her.

He braces himself over her, one hand planted on the bed beside her right shoulder, leaving the left side open and exposed for my view as he slips the other hand between her thighs. She moans. I see her hips moving, and his fingers begin to pump.

"You are tight—very fucking tight," he says. "Let's see if we can open you up a little."

My dick jerks in approval. She frets a little on the bed, but he lowers his lips to her right tit and sucks until she softens and submits.

I've come in her many times in the last night and day, and his vigorous pumping makes the most debauched wet sounds.

His lips pop off a breast. "That's my filthy girl." He looks down the length of her body. "Open your legs wider for me. That's it."

She spreads her legs, opening herself to him as his fingers continue to pump. I see him pull them all the way out, and then, this time, when he pushes in, she arches up off the bed.

"Good girl," he croons. "Let me open you up."

I lean forward on the chair, my breathing unsteady, the blood pounding through my veins as he lowers his lips to a breast again, sucking and nipping, pressing his nose into the underside and then sucking half of it into his mouth.

Her breathing begins to stutter. He stops, and when his touches resume, they are gentler.

"Oh! What? Why did you stop?"

"I don't want you to come yet," he says.

My balls draw tight. Of course, he doesn't. He's an alpha, and this will all be on his terms.

She pouts prettily at him.

"I know, Clara, I know. You have to trust me on this."

He slides his finger inside again, but only one. The filthy wet noises begin again as he slips it in and out, and then it is two fingers, and then it is three.

My amusement flares as I get the distinct impression my wife is trying not to let on how much she likes this. "I think she's playing you," I say, wondering where my loyalties lie to offer this up.

He stills with his finger buried deep, glances across at me, and smirks. "I know. I'm on to her."

She huffs out of breath, and her fingers fist the bedding beside her. "Please don't keep stopping. I'm ready. I'm more than ready."

"Hmm? Do you really think so?"

He directs the weeping tip of his cock at her pussy, and slides the head up and down through her slick folds. I almost feel the moment when he catches her entrance... and pushes.

My breath lodges in my throat, and my balls reach. Somehow, I manage not to fucking come.

And there he stops. She tries to jerk away. He encloses her throat in his fist and pins her still against the bed.

"You were getting impatient, my sweet Clara. Is this not what you want?"

Chapter Eleven

Frederick

The events leading up to this moment are indistinct. There's a woman spread out beneath me. Her long blonde hair falls in waves over her shoulder and against the pillow. She has the kind of sinful body that could bring grown men to their knees. I certainly feel like I have been blessed and poleaxed all at once as I brace above the tiny beta. Her tits are flushed, her nipples hard, and her pussy slick.

There ought to be more preparation. I understand this. And yet, a primitive need is rising within me. One that seeks to claim. I can't fucking claim her. She's a beta, and married. She has a husband—one whom I consider a dear friend. And yet he opened the door to this. Allowed me to step inside. And it is hard to pull back.

I shake my head, trying to clear the fog that clouds my judgment. But it is no fucking use. My hand tightens on her throat, and my cock head breeches the hot welcoming warmth of her pussy. Gods, she is tight. My cock flexes. Her fretting tells me I'm causing her some discomfort, which only makes me want to plow her more.

I am not sane of mind, reverting to a beast-like state, one I have ever striven to mask in the interest of presenting a civilized facade. I am hyper-aware of the woman beneath me and how her pussy flutters around my cock head. Her eyes are a little glassy as she stares up at me. Her legs are spread around my greater bulk.

I lean down and kiss her, and she opens sweetly. Is it presumptuous of me to take her lips and her cunt without checking?

She is not my wife. I'm merely a cock that her husband has chosen to fuck her with, and the act should be done under his terms. I am an exotic titillation. A passing fantasy. A fantasy they have chosen to act out.

Only, alphas are so very driven when they find something that they want. I have forced myself to be blind to this woman, forced myself not to notice her because it is not appropriate for a man to poach another man's wife. Yet here we all are, and as our tongues tangle, I can fool myself and pretend that this is something more.

My heart rate elevates, not only from the sensual pleasure I experience as her pussy strains to swallow the head of my cock, but from the emotional pull. I want to lift my head and roar. I want to do a lot of depraved things to this woman. But most of all, I want to make her mine.

I can't. I know I can't, and yet, that knowledge does not hold me back in the way it should.

Alex is still on the chair, watching. He hasn't told me to stop. He hasn't left the fucking room, either, so I'm thinking he is still on board with allowing this to progress further—the damn fool.

I ought to go over there and shake him for his stupidity,

for presenting this fair woman for me to ravish and defile. She will not be the same when I am done with her. She already has the dazed look of a woman high on alpha pheromones. I will ruin her fucking cunt. I want to. I want to imprint myself on her. I want her to love me and forget him.

I feel ashamed even as I think about these things. Lifting my head, I gaze down at her and try to steady these rampant feelings that are racing through my mind.

A tear escapes the corner of her eyes, and I brush it away with the pad of my thumb, trying to work out what that means.

"Is it... are you all the way in?" she asks fidgeting beneath me.

I pull the tip fully out, and then thrust—*so good*. Her mouth opens to form a silent O, her eyes wide.

"No more than half," I say. That is probably an optimistic assessment, but I believe she will be more encouraged by a half than a more realistic third.

I hear a groan from the other side of the room—it would seem Alex is getting off on this being a struggle for her, and that stirs my dark amusement. It is as though the scent of his arousal is pummeling me from all the way over there.

"Do you like me forcing her?" I glance toward Alex.

He nods. Swallows. Nods again. "Fuck, yes, I do."

"You have a very naughty wife," I say. "She all but goaded me into taking her roughly and sooner than I should." She really didn't. I'm just a bastard, and I'm getting off on this being a challenge as much as her husband is.

"She can take it. She just sometimes makes a little fuss," her traitorous husband says.

I think this is more than a little fuss. I think this is a monstrous strain for the poor beta to take, yet nature has a way, and I feel her softening around me in between the fierce clamping as her body tries to adjust.

I begin to thrust, slow, steady, working deeper, and as I do, I kiss her again, my lips whispering over hers before trailing kisses across her cheek and down the side of her throat. My teeth graze the sensitive skin at the juncture of her shoulder and throat.

My mouth waters with the need to bite, to mark her, and I'm quickly teetering on the brink of madness as I go deeper. Her body trembles under me even as her arms lift to wrap around my neck, and she pulls me in for another kiss.

My hand goes to one tit, squeezing the plump flesh and pinching over her nipple to distract her from what I do. As we kiss, I get deeper still until I'm buried inside her hot, slick channel all the way to the knot. I hold there, letting her get used to the invasion, and all the while, she pulses around me, fidgeting.

"Oh, please move," she says. "Please."

My lips tug up against her throat, and I nip against the flesh; she shudders under me. "I'm going to fuck you now, Clara. This might get a little intense."

I rise up above her. Close the fingers of my right hand around her throat again and take a moment to revel in the stunning image she presents. I keep my touch on her throat light. I don't want to frighten her. But I want her to feel *possessed*.

"Look at that," I say. "Look at how you must stretch around me."

She glances down briefly before she closes her eyes and groans. "Oh, please move, please."

I do, slow at first, her pussy clamping over me with every outward pull and forced to yield as I thrust in again.

Her hot flesh sucks on me, wet and slippery, like a perfect glove caressing my length.

My cock is leaking pre-cum like a tap, and it facilitates my gentle rutting as delicious wet slapping sounds fill the air. "You were made to take an alpha's cock." I don't even stop to think about the filthy words that pour from my lips. The truth is I believe this. I believe in some parallel universe that this woman was destined to be mine.

I blink, trying to regain my equilibrium, to detach myself from what I do, and then I look down at the place where we connect, and a growl escapes my tight control, shifting to a deep, rumbly half-purr of absolute delight and approval.

"God, you are so beautiful. Look at you. Look at how well you take me. I'm so proud of you, Clara. So proud of you for doing this."

I hear a faint moan again from the other side of the room. I realize that this is what Alex wants. He loves and adores his wife. I need to remind myself that he is not giving her to me. He is merely getting off on the fact that I want her, too. "So fucking beautiful, so fucking perfect. And these tits."

They sway as I begin to slam into her with more vigor, bouncing around in the most arresting way. Her face is flushed, and her pretty blue eyes are glassy and barely open.

"Are you going to come for me? Are you going to come all over my cock?" My hand reaches down, my thumb finding the slippery nub of her clit. I watch her expression as I rub over it without mercy, sliding my thumb back and forth, watching the rapture contort her face. "Come for me, woman, come for me now."

Her body turns rigid. Her breath stutters and locks. Then her pussy falls into sweet clenching contractions.

Sweat springs from every pore in my body, and a tell-tale tingle kicks off at the base of my spine. I want to get my fucking knot in, but there is no fucking way. Yet my body reacts of its own accord. My hips pound against hers, the faint swelling of the knot pressing a small way past the slippery entrance as she continues to thrash and come.

I squeeze my fingers over her throat to hold her still, and that sends her absolutely wild.

My hips jackknife, my heart is pounding so hard it feels like it might pound right out of my chest. My mind whites out a little. The feeling of a tight pussy clamping over me all the way to the root has me blinking sweat from my eyes.

"Fuck!"

Alex's hoarse cry from the other side of the room barely penetrates the white-hot rapture coursing through me. I don't move inside her, although the desire to do so is a maddening imperative. I fight it. I don't need to fuck into her for my knot to bloom, just being inside her is enough to tip me over the edge. And it is inside her—nestled right where it was meant to be.

"Oh, oh, oh," she moans. "It's too much. Please!"

Except she's coming again, so I don't do the gentlemanly thing and pull out. No, I pin her still and make her endure, and all the while, I feel my knot flooding with blood, blooming.

Filling.

Stretching.

"Take it," I growl.

My climax is inevitable. I don't know how I've staved it off this long. I feel like cum explodes from my cock. The rush gives me a full-body shudder. My hips jerk erratically, the slight rocking motion of my knot within her tight passage is a torturous kind of pleasure as I dump more cum at the entrance of her womb.

I lean down and kiss her. She's limp. Insensible. A creature of instincts as she writhes upon my knot.

I should have pulled out, come on her belly or tits, on the bed, fucking anywhere. We discussed parameters. We did not discuss where I might come.

It is difficult for an alpha to get a woman pregnant if he does not knot her, but it is possible. It is also possible for a beta to be triggered into becoming fertile if she has been knotted on an alpha's cock. I know they have been trying for a child for a year, and it has not happened yet.

A dark sensation passes over me, one that is unhealthy and possessive, as my cock continues to spew. This woman was made to be a mother. She is sweet and submissive. I revel in the possibility that I might have bred my best friend's wife, might have planted my seed deep in her belly, where it might be nurtured and grow.

Somehow, I rouse myself from this, turning away from this terrible desire toward the man who already claimed her.

The look on his face brings a tightening to my balls and another heady jet of cum.

"You have knotted her," he says.

I can't even get fucking words out. The best I can do is a possessive growl.

She is a twitching mess underneath me. Constantly coming over me, encouraging yet more seed to spill, encouraging me to fill her up. I'm confident I've got her with child, but if I haven't this time, then I will next time.

And there will be a next time because I am far from done with her.

As I look at my friend, I see that he is far from done with me.

He likes us—he is turned fucking on by it.

He swallows.

"She's going to... She's going to feel..."

My lips tug up as I finally find some measure of humor. "Different," I offer.

He chuckles and swipes a hand down his face, then leans back into his chair. His hand goes to his crotch, where he squeezes his cock through his pants. "Gods. Don't. Fuck, I'm going to come, and I'm not even inside her." His expression turns pained, and he shudders with heavy breaths until the moment passes.

I return my attention to the woman beneath me and, leaning down, nibble on her lips. She's open and malleable, *softened* nicely under me. Not that she had any fucking choice. The possessiveness I feel towards her finds some respite now that I have got my seed deep inside her.

Neither of them realizes yet that she is mine, but I am a magnanimous alpha, and I feel inclined toward sharing. As my knot begins to soften a little, I determine that it's time for us to test further the boundaries we have all willfully stumbled over.

Alex

I don't remember stripping my clothes, or the passage between the chair and the bed. A strange, otherworldly sensation settles over me. As I watch him ease his cock from inside her, there is a moment of resistance. She fusses a little, but he pins her still, and then the knot pops free, and a great gush of cum spews out.

I'm standing right next to them, and her legs are spread,

so I have the perfect view. Her pussy clenches, pushing more cum out. I stare down at what he's done. Her little hole is open, all beaten up and puffy.

My throat works again. I try to summon some disgust for what I allowed him to do.

He rises from the bed. His cock is still semi-hard and dripping cum. I want to tell him to get out, to leave us. I'm ravenous for my wife and suddenly greedy to have her all to myself.

"I think you should—"

"Not a fucking chance," he growls. His knee hits the bed at her side, and he sinks down beside her, where he cups her cheek and turns her face. They kiss.

I'm left standing there at the bottom of my own bed, feeling strangely disconnected and yet hyperaware. My cock flexes. Her hips undulate as if encouraging me to fuck her, to fill the hole his massive cock has just left.

The magnitude of what I have done dawns upon me as I stare at my wife's well-used pussy. I have invited an alpha into my home, into our bed, and into my wife's body.

He said it would all be on my terms, but I have a sickening feeling that it is not that way anymore.

I ask myself how I feel about this as I watch them kissing. His big hand is on her breast, squeezing it roughly.

He drags his lips from hers and stills before turning to face me. "What are you waiting for?"

That question comes across like he is the one inviting me to fuck my own wife. I half stagger forward, my knees hitting the edge of the bed. I shake my head, trying to rouse myself, but I'm far too deep into the fog, and my cock, is hard, hot, and desperate to be inside her.

I slide my fingertips through a sticky wetness before

pushing two inside her. I groan. She's wet, open, hot—I've never felt her like this.

I know Frederick's staring at me, but I can't make eye contact. Perhaps he's amused. I don't know if I care, too lost in the moment as my fingers slip out, I line up my cock and sink.

"Gods." I doubt whether my smaller cock even provides stimulation after she has just taken his knot. He said we would build up to that. He said it could take several days or weeks. Not only has he just fucked her with little preparation, but he knotted her and come inside her.

My hips begin to pump erratically. He might have... gotten her with child.

Is that possible? Is that likely?

His growl is approving as I take my wife's hips in my hands and pound into her.

"How does she feel?" he asks casually.

"She feels fucking amazing." The words are punched from my lungs between labored breaths. I'm caught in the throes of some kind of riptide. Her wet openness feels so fucking good around me. I take her without mercy in a way I've never done before. And she is enjoying it, lifting her hips to meet every thrust. Tearing my eyes away from where our flesh slams together, I trail my gaze over her flushed body until my eyes meet hers.

On the bed before me is a creature I don't recognize. Her jaw hangs slack, and her eyes are glassy with lust as her pussy flutters weakly around me.

Sweat breaks out across the surface of my skin. I wanted this, and then I doubted it, and I realize now that I want it more than my next breath. A series of debauched images slam into my mind. Clara sucking me while he watches. Frederick taking her from behind.

Me taking her ass as she sucks him off.

I drag my hips back, pulling out from her, and she gasps and rouses herself up on one elbow. "What?"

"Hands and knees."

Frederick's low chuckle penetrates the fog.

He doesn't hesitate to help, encouraging my wife to roll over onto her hands and knees. Without missing a beat, he reaches for the nightstand, opening the drawer, and rummaging only briefly before he passes the bottle to me.

Her eyes track the passage of the bottle from his hand to mine.

"Wha-what do you need that for, husband?" She stammers over the words. "I don't think I'm—"

"He just knotted you," I say bluntly. "You let him. You enjoyed it. You got fucking off on it. And now it's my turn. My turn to have what I desire."

Her eyes are wide and a little nervous. But I'm a man possessed.

"She will take well to it," Frederick says. He shifts up the bed, sliding in front of her. Fuck, he's going get her to suck him while I take her virgin ass.

"Take your time," he says. "Use plenty of oil." Then he directs her lips towards the weeping cock head in front of her face.

I hear her faint moan before she swallows him down.

Chapter Twelve

Clara

What we began has gone through a metamorphosis. We all wanted this. We were all in agreement. But something has changed. Not that we have rescinded that agreement, for I don't believe any of us have. It is more that we have uncovered what was hidden and unexpected—a dark desire that has a life force of its own.

I get the impression that Frederick has done this with other couples, maybe betas and even omegas too. Jealousy rises swift and potent at the thought of him touching another woman. I suck him deeper, trying to imprint myself on him as my husband trickles oil between the cheeks of my ass, catching it in his fingertips and then thrusting them inside me.

I arch up, my lips popping off Frederick's cock. His fingers tighten in my hair, holding me still, one hand stroking me there. A helpless groan escapes me, and I stare into Frederick's eyes as my husband finger fucks my ass. It burns. But it also feels a dark kind of good. We have skated around this. Alex has wanted this for a while and perhaps I have made more fuss about it than I should.

I was nervous. He assured me many husbands took their wives in this way, yet I wasn't convinced that I believed him. Then the way Frederick discussed it so casually settled a notion in my mind that this was, in fact, an act couples might do.

I'm not afraid anymore, although still a little apprehensive, even as I'm throbbing with arousal. My nervousness is not enough to call a stop, and even so, I don't believe I could. Frederick is very persuasive. I was sure that Alex was about to order him from the room when the alpha growled his counter. *"Don't even think about it."*

My ass clenches around Alex's fingers.

"Try not to clench, sweetheart, lest I need to be rougher with you."

Oh, why does that make me clench tighter? What depravity has taken hold of me? I can't believe I am doing this. I can't believe I just had my husband's best friend's cock in my mouth while my husband prepares my ass for *his* cock.

Frederick's smirk is sinful. Where my husband is regally handsome, Frederick is pure alpha beauty. His cock bobs between us as if to encourage me to resume tending to it.

Alex has worked the oil in and now begins to pump his fingers in a steady rhythm. Frederick is right; it does feel a tingly kind of good. As I let go of fears, my arousal climbs. Then Alex suddenly scissors his fingers inside me, stretching me open, and a gasp pops from my lips.

I try to turn my head, but Frederick tightens his fingers on my hair, holding me at his mercy. "Ah, ah," he says.

"Look at me, love. Let your husband do what he must to prepare your needy little ass. It's going to feel so good when he takes you there. I think you're going to come hard."

There is so much conflict inside me as I submit to the dark, twisty pleasure that blooms. A war takes place in my mind between my love for my husband, and the possessiveness I feel towards the alpha, who is not mine. I digress to wondering and exploring these heightened emotions, even as Alex plays with my body, forcing me to submit to accept his fingers deeper than I have ever done before.

His fingers move faster as he applies more oil. I'm so slippery there that it doesn't matter how I clench, he can pump in and out with ease. I gaze into Frederick's eyes as my bottom tingles inside and out as arousal builds.

A strange, unnatural sense of possession streaks through me as I consider how I am caught between these two very different men. While Alex is loving and encouraging, with a side of playful and wicked, Frederick has a confidence and dominance that is equally irresistible.

I cannot dispute it: even though Frederick is not mine, I want him. Worse, I feel possessive and want to gouge marks in his flesh to ward other lovers off.

He belongs with us.

My arousal rises, my breath turning toward a pant. I can't think straight—can't contain the wild emotions coursing through me.

"You will not fuck other women," I hiss through my teeth, holding Frederick's eyes.

Alex stills with his fingers buried inside me.

Frederick smirks. He brushes his cock tip teasingly over my lips, taunting me. "Shall I not? But how will I ever feel satisfaction without a pretty little beta or omega sucking on my cock again."

"You don't need them."

He arches one brow.

Alex draws a ragged breath. "Clara—"

"Let her speak," Frederick interrupts. "I want to hear what your sweet wife has to say. I believe having your fingers in her ass has provided her with a certain clarity of thought." He brushes my hair behind my ear and cups my cheek. "Why don't I need them, Clara?"

The words catch in my throat as I battle between societal conditioning and what I want. My tongue darts out, and I lap dutifully at the head of his cock. "Because," I say between licks and the swirl of my tongue, "you have me... You have us."

Alex groans lowly, and his fingers resume their dark teasing.

"You are seeking to keep me then, are you?' Frederick goads. "Your personal alpha pet to call on whenever you choose. Is that how it's going to be?"

There is no mistake in the dark undercurrents and the edge of anger. Is he being purposely obtuse?

I swallow the head of his cock, trying to show him all I mean when my words are failing.

He tugs on my hair, pulling me from my prize.

"Is that what I am to you, Clara? Your own personal fuck toy. Nothing but a fat cock and a knot: an alpha who is doomed to live without the joy of love."

"Now is not the fucking time," Alex hisses. "And don't pretend to be confused about what she means."

His fingers suddenly push even deeper, pumping roughly in and out.

I thrash, turning wild.

"Take it," Frederick growls. "I think your *wife* needs

something to distract her lest further inflammatory nonsense pour from her lips."

With a low, filthy curse, Alex's fingers withdraw, and then his cock head presses against my ass. It is so much thicker than his fingers. I jerk, but their hands hold me still, trapping me. Just as I convince myself he can't possibly fit, the bulbous head pops in.

"Oh, it stings!"

It is a little more than a sting—it burns. It is a monstrous strain.

I whimper.

"Hush, love," Frederick says, brushing his thumb over my cheek. When he speaks to me tenderly, I feel the burgeoning hope that he cares, that his cruel words about me using him hide a longing, one I reciprocate, one I dare to hope for.

They also calm me and make me believe I could endure anything if only it would please him.

"Now, open your pretty mouth and suck my cock like a good girl. It will help to distract you from what your husband needs from you."

And I like that too, I want to please my husband who cherishes and loves me, who protects me from the cruelty of the world. I love him so very much. I can be brave, I can do this for him, be good, and take this because it will please him.

I'm a willing prisoner in this. "I will."

Lowering my lips to Frederick's waiting cock, I suck.

Alex grunts. His hands tighten on my hips as he presses deeper into me. I'm so slippery that I can feel him sinking into me with ease, filling me, stretching me.

The taste of Frederick's cock, the copious pre-cum that

leaks, fills my senses and splinters my focus from Alex and the intense burn and strain as he sinks ever deeper into me.

I suck, lap, and lick lovingly on the hot male flesh before me, even as another cock fills my ass.

It doesn't break me.

And as I feel Alex's hips brush against my ass, I realize he is all the way inside me, filling me.

I feel *mastered.*

"Fuck," Frederick says roughly.

My lips pop off his cock as I suck in much-needed air. He tips my chin and holds my eyes.

"How does she feel?"

"Amazing," Alex replies, his voice rough with strain and need. "Slippery and tight. I need to move, but fuck, I think I'm going to come."

"Come if you need to. There will be another time."

The words crash into me.

His lips tug up. "You didn't think this would be enough, did you, sweet Clara? Didn't think I would actually leave to slake my lust somewhere else with someone else when I could be here with you, fucking you, watching your husband fuck you."

My world narrows to this room, this moment, and the two men I share it with.

"Did you not feel it when I was inside you? Did you not feel my seed flooding the entrance to your womb? I have a mind to see you plump with child. Did you know an alpha's knot can trigger a beta's fertility?"

My ears ring. His words feel like they are coming from a great distance. My ass burns, but it also flutters like I might be about to come.

Alex moans weakly and begins to move. Slowly out and slowly in.

And out of the darkness, a strange, twisty pleasure rises.

"She is definitely enjoying this, aren't you, love," Frederick says, pushing three thick fingers into my mouth. I already know I have taken well to this. As Alex moves with greater confidence, my pleasure grows.

Soon, I grunt and groan, lost to the sensations as my husband teaches me the wicked art of love and lust. My entire body is on fire. I'm burning. Everywhere. My pussy aches. Clenching. My ass is fluttering. And then everything spills over into some dark eternal bliss as I spasm around his cock.

"Gods, yes." Alex cries out, his thrusts turn erratic as he pounds into me and then stills with a roar.

A hot flood fills me. I twist and thrash, still coming over his cock. Two sets of hands now hold me for their pleasure, forcing me to endure the darkest, most depraved climax I've experienced in my life.

"Such a good girl," Frederick says. "You have taken to this so well. I believe your husband will need to take you there often. I believe I shall enjoy watching him do as much. I believe now that I have had a taste of a forbidden, and much coveted, beta wife, that I wish to claim her as my own."

Alex groans again. "What the fuck are you saying?"

He's still inside me, still pulsing cum. I know they are staring at one another over me.

Then Alex surprises me when he chuckles. "Your timing could use some work."

Frederick

"I believe my timing is impeccable," I say dryly as he eases out of her body and collapses onto the bed beside her. I draw her forward, settling her beside her husband before I rise from the bed and head over to the adjoining bathroom. I dampen the cloth and return to the bedroom where I find their heads are pressed together and sticky bodies entwined.

The cloud of jealousy is sudden and rampant as I pause at the bottom of the bed, seeing all their love.

Only there is no place for jealousy here. I am the spare dick, so to speak, who is seeking to be something more. I told myself I would fuck off if he told me to and yet it's already too late. I'm invested. A fucking army of orcs couldn't drag me from this room.

He watches but offers no comment as I part her thighs and clean her up with gentle dabs. His eyes hold that gleam again that tells me he likes me tending to her, likes seeing my hands on her.

I pass him the cloth. He cleans himself up and then drops it onto the floor. I rake a hand through my hair. My cock is hard and hungry for her cunt, her lips, her small hand brushing against me would probably be enough.

She glances back and holds out her hand to me. My dick jerks like she is offering to jack me off—she isn't but, I exhale a low purr because that hand offers so much more than the promise of quick relief.

It offers hope, a connection my lonely soul wants to embrace. How strange to have been so lonely amid so many offers of companionship and more. Rebecca was not the only omega the high king permitted me to court. It is only now, as I stare down at this forbidden fruit, that I understand why. Today, I see Clara as far more than my best friend's wife. I have opened a door and allowed burgeoning feelings to thrive.

"An alpha is ever a determined beast when he wants something," I say.

"I know," Alex says. "I understand."

"Do you?"

"Take her hand, Frederick. You're upsetting her. I don't care how big you are, I will kick you out of my fucking house if you upset my wife."

My lips tug up. Those blunt words are the reason why I call Alex my best friend.

I take her hand because I see in his face and hear in his words a deeper understanding of love. I can't be sure who started this anymore, was it Alex, or was he merely acting on instinct and hidden feelings I was previously blind to? He would do anything to please his wife; her physical and emotional happiness are all that matters to him.

Even in this.

I kiss the back of her hand, and then, with a sense of inevitability, I lie down behind her.

"She is possessive of me," I say, with no small amount of pride in my voice.

Alex chuckles. "Yeah, I did get that part."

"I don't want him to go," she says softly, trailing kisses along Alex's throat.

He groans and presses a chaste kiss to her forehead. "I know, sweetheart. I don't want him to go either, nor do I want to imagine him fucking someone else. Not when he is yours now. Isn't he?"

Her hand tightens over mine. "Yes."

My chest swells and a deep rumbly purr escapes. I blink away the strange sting at the back of my eyes. Warmth spreads through me, getting all mixed up with the sharp arousal I still feel. Her scent fills my lungs—*so familiar*. Closing my eyes, I lower my lips to the juncture of her shoulder and throat and nip.

"There," Alex says. "I don't know how this shall work, only that the three of us together feels right and we should not burden ourselves trying to force matters or conform. While it's not unheard of for an alpha to be with a beta, it is perhaps a little unusual for him to steal another man's wife."

I hear the humor in his voice, but I still grumble, "I'm not fucking stealing your wife."

"No," he agrees. "You are sharing her. If anything, that might meet with greater disapproval."

"I don't care what anybody thinks," Clara says, pressing a kiss to her husband's cheek before she peeks back at me.

"Do not give me that look, woman," I say.

"What look?"

I'm not falling for the fake innocence she seeks to project. Not anymore. "The look that says you want to be fucked."

Alex groans as though in great pain. "My cock is fucking raw. I've done nothing but fuck her for the last day and night since you arrived. I've just taken her sweet ass." He huffs out a breath and gestures toward his cock. "Now I'm hardening again."

"Best get used to it," I say, skimming my hand over her hips and down her thigh until I reach the juncture of her knee. I draw her leg up and out, repositioning myself so that my cock nestles against her slick cunt. "Guide me into your wife."

There is a brief moment of hesitation before his eyes lower. His groan is one of defeat as he grasps my cock and guides me where I need to go. "Gods, that looks obscene and hot all at once." His fingers linger, rubbing gentle circles against her clit as I slowly push into her.

She arches up and groans—I could listen to that breathy note of pleasure forever and never tire. Reaching back, she cups the back of my head.

I kiss her throat, pulling her leg a little higher as I begin to thrust.

"If I'm not very much mistaken, I think your sweet wife is becoming fertile," I say.

Her pussy clenches over me in the most arresting way.

"Fuck! Do you think...?" —he swallows— "We've tried for a year."

"I would very much like to see Clara with child," I say, picking up my strokes, hearing those delicious wet noises as I shuttle in and out. "How would you feel if it was mine?"

"Happy," he says, without even the briefest hesitation. "So fucking happy."

Epilogue

Six months later...

Clara

"Are those fresh strawberries?" Frederick asks as he enters the dining room where Alex and I are eating breakfast.

Not that I'm eating a lot of breakfast. The truth is I'm playing with my food, moving the fruit around my plate while thinking about my husband and what he did with his wicked tongue this morning before we even roused ourselves from bed.

"They are," Alex replies. "Why, did you want some?"

"No." Frederick shakes his head and draws out the chair next to me. He sits, plucking me from my seat as though I'm nothing but a little doll and not the size of a small, plump cow. He sits me on the table before him, sliding his chair forward and leaving me no choice but to open my legs around him.

A squeak escapes my lips as he pushes up the hem of the scandalously short gown that he insists I wear when we are not expecting visitors to our house.

We don't have visitors often, which means I am mostly dressed this way.

Frederick wiggles his eyebrows suggestively at me. "I was going to assist your wife in eating her food. She has been very picky of late." His eyes land on my round belly.

I'm in the latter stage of my second trimester, and they are both a little obsessed with my expanding waistline. One did not realize a plump belly would be a source of both pride and erotic interest.

He cups the mound and leans it to kiss it. "Gods, you have a beautiful wife," he says agreeably to Alex.

I glance over my shoulder at my husband, who grins. "And you have a stunning mate."

They love to do this, to both praise me as though I belong to the other one. It is a little wicked game they play like I am a forbidden fruit, one they both secretly covet.

Frederick's hands move to my breasts, and he squeezes them together. "Are your wife's tits getting bigger, do you think?"

"For certain," Alex agrees. He rises from his chair under the pretense of refilling his coffee cup from the pot.

At the same time, he's also staring at what we do, his eyes hungry.

My husband and my mate are always hungry for me. I'm the luckiest woman in all the lands to have such fine men attentive to my every need.

"Lie back, love," Frederick encourages, with a gentle press of his hand before he lifts the hem of my gown.

Alex brings his coffee over to stand beside Frederick, watching with heated interest as his best friend uses his finger and thumb to part the lips of my pussy, holding me open lewdly for their review.

"Pretty," Alex says, eyes hooded as he takes a sip of his coffee.

Frederick selects an uneaten strawberry from my plate. Expression darkly intense, he slides it through my slick pussy, making sure to catch it against my swollen clit with every pass.

"That strawberry's looking tastier by the moment," Alex says thickly.

"Isn't it just?" Frederick agrees.

I live in a perpetual state of arousal. Sometimes they enjoy me together. But more often, they take turns to either pleasure me or watch me be pleasured. Given my husband's attention this morning, I am well primed, so it does not take long before my breath hitches and my pussy flutters in hopeful anticipation.

Just when I think I'm about to come, Frederick lifts the strawberry and presents it to my lips.

"Open up, mate, and eat your strawberry like a good girl."

I squirm a little. He brushes it over my lips, and helplessly, I open. I taste myself on it as I bite down, and then the sweetness of the strawberry explodes across my tongue.

Alex clears his throat. "I think she might be hungry for more than just a strawberry."

"Do you think so?" Frederick says, brows tugging together, enrapt, as I chew slowly on the succulent fruit.

"For certain," Alex says. "My wife sometimes needs a little more. It's her pregnancy, it makes her terribly needy. It's a very delicate subject, but I know I have your discretion."

"Of course," Frederick says. "If there is some way I can

assist with her predicament, which I understand she cannot help, you can count on me. I won't be shocked. No matter how filthy or depraved."

The words *filthy* and *depraved* come out like a caress.

"Oh, I think you might be when I tell you my sweet wife craves an alpha's knot."

His words, with their element of taboo, are like liquid heat spreading over my intimate places.

I admit there was a period of adjustment as we learned to navigate our ménage à trois. But that time is behind us, and we are very much aligned and enamored with what we now share. I am wearing a scandalous dress at Frederick's insistence, and without panties at Alex's determining. They both love me vigorously and frequently, making a mockery of this conversation.

Frederick's eyes darken further, I'm certain he is going to rise, take down his pants, and knot me how I need. Then afterward, when I'm all open and well-used, my husband will enjoy me because that is how he likes me best.

"Hmmm. Are you sure about that?" Frederick asks, plucking a... raspberry from my plate.

He's not going to use that... is he?

Of course, he does.

Alex chuckles.

I groan and fling an arm dramatically across my face. "Oh, just knot me already."

"Knot you? Did I hear that right?"

I peek under my arm as Frederick turns to Alex in question.

"I believe you did," Alex says. "I believe my wife might want you to fuck her right here on the dining table while the patio doors lay open, and anyone might see."

Frederick, the teasing beast, slides the small, inadequate raspberry over my pussy, making me needy and urgent.

"She definitely needs cock," Alex says, bluntly.

"Yes, I'm getting that impression now, too," Frederick says, smirking. "You have a very needy wife."

"And you have a very filthy mate," Alex agrees, his grin turning wicked as he draws my arm away and removes my hiding place. Maintaining eye contact, he tugs down the bodice of my gown. "It is for the best that there are two of us so that she may always and forever have exactly what she needs."

The air leaves me on a breathy moan as he closes his lips over my distended nipple and sucks.

With a growl, Frederick rises and pops the slick raspberry into his mouth. "Fucking delicious," he rumbles, already reaching for the buckles of his pants.

I cry out with joy as his thick cock penetrates me all the way to the root, the knot already a little swollen with his need. There he fucks me, the plates and cutlery bouncing about under his vigorous rutting until I'm nothing but a writhing mess and begging for his knot. My pussy throbs, and the little nerves that never really have the chance to quiet flare under the delectable stretch of his fat cock and blooming knot.

A climax rips through me, shooting sparks through my nipples and all the way down to my pussy as I clench around his thick, perfect flesh in sweet, rhythmic waves.

Taking a firm grip on my hips, he slows his thrusts, working the thick knot in and out, prolonging the climax until I'm hoarse from begging for a respite, for more—I know not what I even say.

Finally, he knots me, and I hang in a state of perpetual bliss, fluttering over his thick length.

"You're going to feel so good around my cock," Alex growls beside my ear. "I love how softened you are. How you can't stop coming after my best friend is done with you."

Fingers entwined in Alex's hair, I drag his lips to mine, and we share a hot kiss full of tangling tongues and breathy gasps. His urgency is a potent aphrodisiac and one I am addicted to, one I couldn't live without any more than I could live without my alpha mate.

I don't have to choose between them, for they love to share me as much as I love to be shared.

Here, within earthly bounds, I find my own heaven with my wicked beta husband and my sinful alpha mate.

❦

Did you enjoy The Coveted Beta? Please consider leaving a review. Authors love reviews!

What is next from Coveted Prey? How about an extra spicy bear shifter story... Beauty and the Bears!

For free short stories, please check out BOOKS | FREE READS on my website www.AuthorLVLane.com

Enjoying my writing? You can find my latest WIP in serial format by becoming a Patron https://reamstories.com/ lvlane

Also by L.V. Lane

Coveted Prey

The Controllers

Ten book dark sci-fi omegaverse series.

Book One: The Awakening

Mate for the Alien Master

Four book alien romance.

Book one: Punished

About the Author

In a secret garden hidden behind a wall of shrubs and trees, you'll find L.V. Lane's writing den, where she crafts adventures in fantastical worlds.

Best known for spicy adventures...Magical and mythical creatures, wolf shifters, and alphas of every flavor who give sweet and feisty omegas and heroines a guaranteed HEA, she also writes the occasional character-driven hard sci-fi full of political intrigue and action.

Subscribe to my mailing list at my website for the latest news: www.AuthorLVLane.com

Printed in Great Britain
by Amazon

43108652R00067